The Colony of New Hampshire

A Primary Source History

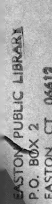

PowerKids Press
PRIMARY SOURCE

Melody S. Mis

To Bobby, who painted my world yellow

Published in 2007 by The Rosen Publishing Group, Inc.
29 East 21st Street, New York, NY 10010

First Edition

Editor: Jennifer Way
Book Design: Ginny Chu
Layout Design: Julio Gil
Photo Researcher: Nicole DiMella

Photo Credits: Cover, p. 20 © North Wind/North Wind Picture Archives; p. 4 © Royalty-Free/Corbis; p. 4 (inset) General Research Division, The New York Public Library, Astor, Lenox, and Tilden Foundations; p. 6 © The Image Works Archives; pp. 6 (inset), 8 (inset), 12 (inset) New Hampshire Historical Society; p. 8 The Art Archive/Culver Pictures; p. 10 Library of Congress, Prints and Photographs Division; p. 10 (inset) © Mary Evans Picture Library/The Image Works; p. 12 © Baldwin H. Ward & Kathryn C. Ward/Corbis; p. 14 The Granger Collection, New York; p. 14 (inset) Library of Congress, Manuscript Division; pp. 16, 16 (inset) Library of Congress, Rare Book and Special Collections Division; p. 18 Ann Ronan Picture Library/HIP/The Image Works; pp. 18 (inset), 20 (inset) Emmet Collection, Miriam and Ira D. Wallach Division of Art, Prints and Photographs, The New York Public Library, Astor Lenox and Tilden Foundations.

Library of Congress Cataloging-in-Publication Data

Mis, Melody S.
  The colony of New Hampshire : a primary source history / by Melody S. Mis.— 1st ed.
      p. cm. — (The primary source library of the thirteen colonies and the Lost Colony)
  Includes index.
  ISBN 1-4042-3435-7 (library binding)
  1. New Hampshire—History—Colonial period, ca. 1600–1775—Juvenile literature. 2. New Hampshire—History—1775–1865—Juvenile literature. 3. New Hampshire—History—Colonial period, ca. 1600–1775—Sources—Juvenile literature. 4. New Hampshire—History—1775–1865—Sources—Juvenile literature. I. Title. II. Series.
  F37.M57 2007
  974.2'02—dc22

                                    2005025627

Manufactured in the United States of America

Contents

This map of the East Coast was made about 50 years after the English first settled New Hampshire. Inset: One of the things explorers hoped to bring back to England was a plant called sassafras. The plant can be used for dyes and soaps. It can also be used as a flavoring, or it can be made into a tea.

Discovering New Hampshire

In 1623, New Hampshire became England's third colony in North America. New Hampshire's first **inhabitants** were Native Americans. The Pennacook were living on New Hampshire's coast when the first European set foot there.

The first European to explore New Hampshire was the Englishman Martin Pring. He landed near present-day Portsmouth in 1603, while searching for a plant called sassafras to bring back to England. Pring did not find it, so he returned to England.

In 1614, John Smith visited New Hampshire to see if it would be a good place for a colony. Smith had helped settle Jamestown, Virginia, which was England's first colony in North America. Smith wrote a book about New England, of which New Hampshire is a part. This led to people becoming interested in settling there.

Strawberry Banke, shown in this picture, changed its name to Portsmouth in 1653. This new name was chosen because the settlement was at the mouth of the Piscataqua River. Inset: John Mason is shown here splitting off land and naming it New Hampshire. Mason spent his own money to help build and establish New Hampshire, although he died before he could visit it.

England Founds Its Third Colony

New Hampshire was founded as a business enterprise. In 1620, James I, king of England, gave a **charter** to a group of English businessmen. The businessmen gave a land grant of 6,000 acres (2,400 ha) to Dave Thompson in 1622. They told him to plant grapes, to trade with the Native Americans, and to establish a fishing business. The Englishmen hoped to make money from these businesses. Thompson and his settlers landed in New Hampshire in 1623, and they founded the town of Rye.

In 1622, the English businessmen also gave a piece of land to John Mason. Mason named it New Hampshire, after Hampshire County in England. In 1630, he sent colonists to New Hampshire. They called their settlement Strawberry Banke, because there were strawberries growing there. This village later became known as Portsmouth.

The governing Puritans asked people who did not agree with the Puritans' rules to leave the Massachusetts settlement. Many of the people who left Massachusetts came to New Hampshire. Inset: Passaconaway, chief of the Pennacook, worked to have peaceful relations with the New Hampshire colonists.

Settling New Hampshire

In 1638, two groups of people from the Massachusetts Bay Colony settled in New Hampshire, where they founded the towns of Exeter and Hampton. Many of these people had been asked to leave Massachusetts by the **Puritans**, who governed that colony. These people did not agree with the Puritans' rules.

When settlers moved to New Hampshire, the nearby Pennacook were friendly neighbors. The chief of the Pennacook was called Passaconaway, which means "child of the bear." Passaconaway told his followers not to fight with the colonists. The Pennacook taught the settlers many useful things. The Pennacook showed them how to plant their crops. They taught them how to keep meat fresh by covering it with snow. They taught them how to build boats and how to use plants to treat illnesses.

New Hampshire's capital, Portsmouth, became an important city for businesses such as boat making and fishing. Inset: Charles II was the king of England from 1660 until 1685. He made New Hampshire a royal colony in 1680.

New Hampshire Joins Massachusetts

By the mid-1600s, New Hampshire was a small colony. Massachusetts, to the south, was larger and better organized. In 1641, New Hampshire joined the Massachusetts Bay Colony. It remained part of Massachusetts until 1680.

There were many differences between the colonists in Massachusetts and the colonists in New Hampshire. The Puritans in Massachusetts were **stricter** than were the people in New Hampshire. This meant that there were sometimes disagreements about how to run the colony.

In 1680, King Charles II of England separated New Hampshire from Massachusetts. He made New Hampshire a royal colony and named Portsmouth its capital. He also gave the colony an **elected assembly**. New Hampshire remained a royal colony until the **American Revolution**.

Rogers' Rangers were the most famous of the local military groups formed to help the British fight in the French and Indian War. These groups were valued for their ability to live in the wilderness and to fight battles in heavily wooded areas. Inset: Robert Rogers lived from 1731 until 1795. The fighting style he popularized was later printed as Rogers' Ranging Rules.

New Hampshire Grows

New Hampshire's businesses were based on its **natural resources**, which included fish, fur, and lumber. These products were in great demand in Europe.

While New Hampshire's businesses were growing, Britain and France began to fight for control of the colonies in the **French and Indian War**. Britain needed help for the war effort. New Hampshire's popular governor, Benning Wentworth, sent money and some of the colony's best soldiers. New Hampshirites were so good at fighting that the British asked them to form a special military force. They were called Rogers' Rangers after their leader, Robert Rogers. The Rangers helped the British win the war.

Robert Rogers was born in 1731. Rogers learned about his surroundings from Native Americans who lived nearby. In 1755, he joined the British during the French and Indian War. He was a good soldier and soon became a leader. Rogers was asked to form a special army group called Rogers' Rangers. By the end of the war, Rogers had become one of New Hampshire's most famous soldiers.

13

Georgii III. Regis.

CAP. XI.

An Act to repeal an Act made in the last Session of Parliament, intituled, *An Act for granting and applying certain Stamp Duties, and other Duties, in the British Colonies and Plantations in America, towards further defraying the Expences of defending, protecting, and securing the same ; and for amending such Parts of the several Acts of Parliament relating to the Trade and Revenues of the said Colonies and Plantations, as direct the Manner of determining and recovering the Penalties and Forfeitures therein mentioned.*

WHEREAS an Act was passed in the last Session of Parliament, intituled, An Act for granting and applying certain Stamp Duties, and other Duties, in the British Colonies and Plantations in America, towards further defraying the Expences of defending, protecting, and securing the same ; and for amending such Parts of the several Acts of Parliament relating to the Trade and Revenues of the said Colonies and Plantations, as direct the Manner of determining and recovering the Penalties and Forfeitures therein mentioned : And whereas the Continuance of the said Act would be attended with many

From The Stamp Act

"An Act for granting and applying certain Stamp Duties, and other Duties, in the British colonies and Plantations in America, towards further defraying the Expenses of defending, protecting, and securing the same . . ."

This opening part of the Stamp Act explains that a tax will be enacted on the British colonies in North America. The purpose of the tax is to pay for guarding the colonies during the French and Indian War.

This picture shows a Stamp Act protest in New Hampshire. It shows a dummy of the New Hampshire stamp agent being hanged. This was a common protest action against the hated act. Inset: The Stamp Act, shown here, was passed in 1765 and was repealed, or ended, in 1766.

Britain Taxes the Colonies

After the French and Indian War ended in 1763, Britain needed to find a way to pay back the money it had borrowed from other countries. Since the war benefited the colonies, Britain believed they should pay for it through taxes.

In 1764, Britain taxed the colonies on sugar, coffee, and silk cloth. When Britain passed the Stamp Act in 1765, the colonists **protested**. The Stamp Act stated that the colonists had to buy a stamp for all paper goods. Colonists in Portsmouth protested by hanging dummies of the stamp seller on trees. This scared the stamp seller, who quit his job and left town. Britain repealed, or ended, the Stamp Act in 1766, but it passed other laws that taxed the colonies on other products. It would be a few years before the colonists got angry enough to begin thinking about becoming independent from Britain.

From Boston Port Act of 1774

"The following Act of Parliament . . . is printed for the information of the merchants of Great Britain and Ireland trading to North America. An act to discontinue in such manner and for such time . . . the landing or shipping of goods . . . at the town, and within the harbour of Boston . . ."

The opening part of the Boston Port Act tells merchants who trade in North America that they are not to do any business in Boston.

This 1789 picture shows the Boston Tea Party. Inset: The Boston Port Act closed Boston's harbor. This action led New Hampshirites to boycott, or refuse to buy, British tea to show the neighboring colony that they were on their side. Instead they made what they called Liberty Tea. It was made from different types of plants, such as sassafras.

Taxation Without Representation

During the early 1770s, Britain continued passing new laws and taxes on the colonies. This angered the colonists because they were not **represented** in **Parliament**. That means they had no lawful way either to protest against or to consent to laws that had an effect on them. Therefore they did not believe that Britain should tax them or pass laws that affected them.

After the Boston Tea Party in 1773, Britain closed Boston's harbor. New Hampshirites protested this action. When British ships landed in Portsmouth with a load of tea, the colonists boycotted. That means they refused to buy the tea. The New Hampshirites were tired of Britain taxing them without their approval. Soon they would use the phrase "taxation without representation" as their battle cry for independence.

In December 1774, John Sullivan led a group of patriots to take gunpowder from Fort William and Mary. The gunpowder went to patriots throughout New Hampshire. Inset: John Sullivan lived from 1740 until 1795. He was a military leader, and he served in the Continental Congress.

New Hampshire Prepares for War

In September 1774, John Sullivan and Nathaniel Folsom from New Hampshire met with leaders from the other colonies in Philadelphia, Pennsylvania, to form the First Continental Congress. Congress sent a list of their objections to Britain. Britain replied by sending troops to New England. Before Britain's troops arrived, John Sullivan led around 500 **patriots** to Fort William and Mary in Portsmouth. They stole the guns and gunpowder stored there. It was one of the colonies' first military actions against Britain.

When the American Revolution began in April 1775, New Hampshire's John Stark and his soldiers entered the war. One month later Sullivan and John Langdon represented New Hampshire at the Second Continental Congress in Philadelphia.

John Stark led a group of New Hampshire soldiers who helped guard Vermont in the Battle of Bennington in August 1777. This patriot win helped weaken British forces, which led to the important patriot win at Saratoga in October 1777. Inset: John Stark was another of New Hampshire's famous patriot generals. Stark lived from 1728 until 1822.

New Hampshire and the American Revolution

On July 4, 1776, Josiah Bartlett, Matthew Thornton, and William Whipple signed the **Declaration of Independence**, which stated that the colonies were free of British rule. Once the declaration had been signed, the colonies had to keep their freedom by fighting for it.

During the American Revolution, New Hampshire was the only colony where there were no battles. The colony, however, provided the army with soldiers and supplies. Army leaders John Sullivan and John Stark became famous for their bravery during the battles at Trenton, New Jersey, and Saratoga, New York. About 100 **privateers** from New Hampshire helped keep the British from supplying their troops by blocking Colonial ports. The Americans won the war when they beat the British at the Battle of Yorktown in Virginia on October 19, 1781.

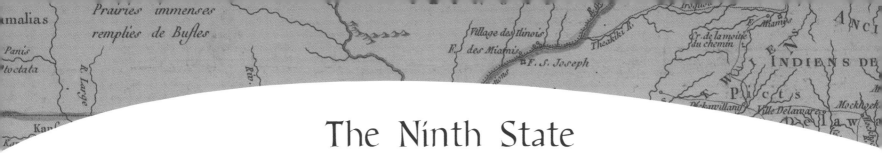

The Ninth State

The American Revolution officially ended in 1783, when the United States and Britain signed the Treaty of Paris. Then the 13 colonies had to govern themselves as one nation.

To form a new government, the Constitutional Convention was held in Philadelphia in 1787. John Langdon and Nicholas Gilman represented New Hampshire. They helped create the U.S. **Constitution**, which still governs the United States today.

The Constitution had to be adopted by nine of the colonies before it went into effect. Once a colony adopted the Constitution, it became a state. The Constitution took effect on June 21, 1788, when New Hampshire became the ninth state to adopt it.

Glossary

American Revolution (uh-MER-uh-ken reh-vuh-LOO-shun) Battles that soldiers from the colonies fought against Britain for freedom, from 1775 to 1783.

charter (CHAR-tur) An official agreement giving someone permission to do something.

Constitution (kon-stih-TOO-shun) The basic rules by which the United States is governed.

Declaration of Independence (deh-kluh-RAY-shun UV in-duh-PEN-dints) An official announcement signed on July 4, 1776, in which American colonists stated they were free of British rule.

elected assembly (ih-LEKT-ed uh-SEM-blee) A meeting with a lot of people who were chosen by their peers to attend.

French and Indian War (FRENCH AND IN-dee-un WOR) The battles fought between 1754 and 1763 by England, France, and Native Americans for control of North America.

inhabitants (in-HA-buh-tents) People who live in a certain place.

natural resources (NA-chuh-rul REE-sors-ez) Things in nature that can be used by people.

Parliament (PAR-leh-ment) The group in England that makes the country's laws.

patriots (PAY-tree-uts) American colonists who believed in separating from British rule.

privateers (pry-vuh-TEERZ) Armed ships allowed by a government to attack enemy ships.

protested (pruh-TEST-ed) Acted out in disagreement of something.

Puritans (PYUR-ih-tenz) Members of a religious group in England who moved to America during the seventeenth century.

represented (reh-prih-ZENT-ed) Stood for.

stricter (STRIKT-er) More careful in following a rule or making others follow it than other people are.

Index

Primary Sources

Page 4. Map of Mid-Atlantic and New England. 1673, Hugo Allard, Donald Heald Rare Books, Prints & Maps, New York, New York. **Page 6. Inset.** Mason and Gorges divide land. Woodcut, New Hampshire Historical Society, Concord, New Hampshire. **Page 8. Inset.** Passaconaway. Etching, seventeenth century, New Hampshire Historical Society, Concord, New Hampshire. **Page 10.** *View of Portsmouth, New Hampshire from across the Piscataqua River.* Aquatint and etching, 1780, Joseph F. W. Des Barres, Library of Congress. New Hampshire Historical Society, Concord, New Hampshire. **Page 12. Inset.** Robert Rogers. After Thomas Hart 1776 mezzotint, Corbis, New Hampshire Historical Society, Concord, New Hampshire. **Page 14. Inset.** The Stamp Act. 1766, printed by Mark Baskett, Library of Congress, Manuscript Division, Washington, D.C. **Page 16.** *Boston Tea Party.* Engraving, 1789, W. D. Cooper, Library of Congress Rare Book and Special Collections Division, Washington, D.C. **Page 16. Inset.** Boston Port Act. April 7, 1774, Library of Congress, Washington, D.C. **Page 18. Inset.** John Sullivan. Wood engraving, eighteenth century, New York Public Library, New York, New York. **Page 20. Inset.** John Stark. Wood engraving, circa 1780, New York Public Library, New York, New York.

Web Sites

Due to the changing nature of Internet links, PowerKids Press has developed an online list of Web sites related to the subject of this book. This site is updated regularly. Please use this link to access the list: www.powerkidslinks.com/pstclc/newhamps/